P9-DNR-640

BY JAKE MADDOX

illustrated by Sean Tiffany

text by Anastasia Suen

Librarian Reviewer
Chris Kreie
Media Specialist, Eden Prairie Schools, MN
MS in Information Media, St. Cloud State University, MN

Reading Consultant
Mary Evenson
Middle School Teacher, Edina Public Schools, MN
MA in Education, University of Minnesota

STONE ARCH BOOKS
Minneapolis San Diego

Impact Books are published by Stone Arch Books
151 Good Counsel Drive, P.O. Box 669
Mankato, Minnesota 56002
www.stonearchbooks.com

Library of Congress Cataloging-in-Publication Data
Maddox, Jake.
    BMX Bully / by Jake Maddox; illustrated by Sean Tiffany.
    p. cm. — (Impact Books. A Jake Maddox Sports Story)
    Summary: Eleven-year-old Matt wants to make the Evergreen
Racing Team but his chances are seriously threatened when a new boy
moves to town and resorts to cheating in order to win.
    ISBN-13: 978-1-59889-059-4 (library binding)
    ISBN-10: 1-59889-059-X (library binding)
    ISBN-13: 978-1-59889-236-9 (paperback)
    ISBN-10: 1-59889-236-3 (paperback)
    [1. Bicycle racing—Fiction. 2. Cheating—Fiction.] I. Tiffany,
Sean, ill. II. Title. III. Series: Maddox, Jake. Impact Books (Stone
Arch Books) Jake Maddox Sports Story.
PZ7.S94343Bx 2007
[Fic]—dc22   2006006074

Art Director: Heather Kindseth
Cover Graphic Designer: Heather Kindseth
Interior Graphic Designer: Kay Fraser

1 2 3 4 5 6 11 10 09 08 07 06

Printed in the United States of America

Table of Contents

CHAPTER 1

Evergreen

The sun was shining on the first day of the BMX racing season. Matt Daniels was looking at the racing sheets. The names of the racers were posted by age on the board at the Evergreen Racetrack.

I wonder who Tyler Mason is, thought Matt. He wasn't here last year.

Then Matt saw a notice tacked on the board.

Only the top rider in each age group will be on the Evergreen Racing Team.

What is that all about? Matt wondered. Dad never had that rule when he ran the track. But now his Dad was overseas and wouldn't be back for nine months.

Matt rode his bike over to the starting gate. The track looked in good condition. Matt watched the twelve-year-olds mount their bikes. Their front tires were facing downhill, touching the gate.

Bang! The gate dropped forward and the riders rode over it and down the hill.

Once the riders were down the hill, the official raised the gate again. A tall boy with black hair rode up to the gate next to Matt. He must be that new kid, Tyler, Matt thought.

"You won't be wearing that Evergreen Racing Team shirt very long," said Tyler.

"Why?" said Matt.

"I was state champion before we moved here," said Tyler. "I'm just letting you know how it's going to go down."

"I see," said Matt. He looked at Tyler's face. The boy's eyes looked hard and mean. "My father owns this track now," said Tyler. "He's spent a lot of money cleaning up your father's mess."

"He what?" said Matt. Matt didn't need this just before the race.

Bang! The gate dropped and the race was on.

Chapter 2

First Moto

Matt rode over the starter's gate and down the hill. Tyler was already ahead of him!

What was that about his dad? thought Matt as he rode up the first jump. It couldn't be true. Tyler was just trying to distract me. And it worked. He's over the second hill already!

The other boys were behind Matt, but they were picking up speed.

I could lose this race if I'm not careful!

Matt pedaled toward the second hill as fast as he could.

After the jump, Matt was closer, but Tyler was still ahead.

Tyler hit the third hill as Matt rode up to it.

Matt flew over the third hill. He landed just behind Tyler.

A few more feet and they reached the first turn. It was a left turn, curved up into a bank.

Matt rode to the top of the curve. If I ride high enough, I can pass him when I come out of the turn, he thought.

"Hey!" yelled Tyler as Matt passed him.

Two hills were next. The second one was higher than the first. Matt rolled up the first hill and jumped. Airborne!

Matt landed on the second hill, pedaled up, and jumped again.

He raced into the second turn. Matt rolled high again and leaned into it, trying to move even faster.

Wham! Tyler rammed his front tire into Matt's back tire. Matt's bike wobbled.

Whack! Tyler reached out and pushed Matt.

Matt and his bike flew over the top of the curve. The official by the turn looked at Matt lying on the ground, but he didn't say anything.

What's wrong with that official? thought Matt.

Pushing was against the rules and so was ramming.

Matt picked himself up and got back on his bike. He rode it up over the top of the curve. I'm going to finish this race!

Matt rode out of the second curve and jumped the two tabletops in the next straightaway. Matt picked up speed on the final curve. He almost flew over the four rolling jumps, and then he crossed the finish line.

The race is over, and I'm last. Dead last, thought Matt. No points for being last. How am I going to stay on the team if I don't have any points?

Chapter 3

Second Moto

Matt put his helmet on and rolled his bike up to lane one. It was time for the second race. Matt looked down the line. Tyler was in lane six this time.

Bang!

The gate went down, and Matt pedaled as fast as he could. He cleared the first three low rolls in seconds.

Matt could hear the other riders coming up behind him.

The first turn was just ahead. I have to make it there before Tyler, Matt thought.

Faster and faster he pedaled. Then he leaned hard and went through the bottom of the turn. It was shorter at the bottom, so he pulled out first.

"Hey!" Tyler yelled.

Matt rolled up the first tabletop and flew over it. He didn't even land on it!

The two rising hills were next. They ended at the next turn. Matt leaned forward as he pedaled and jumped up! He could hear the other riders behind him.

At the beginning of the second turn, someone hit his back wheel.

Matt tried to straighten out his bike and wham! Another rider hit him, and they both fell over. As Matt went down, he saw Tyler ride past.

Matt untangled himself from the other kid's bike and got back on his own. The other riders are already on the last straightaway.

Matt began pedaling. He jumped the two flat tabletops and turned left. Then he came to the three hill jumps. Matt could hear the other rider coming up behind him. Matt pedaled faster.

As the other rider came closer, Matt jumped higher. Around the last curve he flew, and then it was the last straightaway.

Matt rode full speed into the four low rises and made it through all of them. He crossed the finish line fifth, not last.

"Woo, boy! You are good," said Tyler. "Now you're only second to last, not dead last."

Matt ignored him and rode off.

"Mr. Big Shot can't take it," Tyler yelled after him.

Not from you, I won't, thought Matt. You only win because you cheat.

Chapter 4

Third Moto

Matt rode up the starter's hill for the third race. He was in lane three. Tyler was in lane four.

Matt closed his eyes and took a deep breath. He had to win this race!

Bang! The gate dropped.

Matt pedaled down the starter's hill as fast as he could. Tyler was right next to him.

Tyler kept pace with Matt as he began the first of the three rolling hills. The two riders went over the first hill together.

The second hill came right after the first. Then Tyler twisted his back wheel and tried to hit Matt again.

Matt was ready. He dodged the tire.

Whoof! The bikes hit the dirt.

Rolling hill number three was just two pedals away. Matt slowed down and let Tyler pass. Tyler rolled high into the curve, trying to pick up speed. Matt rolled into the bottom of the first curve. His path was shorter, so when he came out of the turn, he was ahead of Tyler!

The tabletop hill was next. Tyler was still in midair when Matt landed. Matt started the first of the two rising hills.

"Hey, you!" yelled Tyler, but Matt didn't turn around. He could hear Tyler coming up behind him. Matt jumped the first hill and landed. Thump! Tyler was right behind him.

Matt started up the second hill. Wham! Tyler hit Matt's tire from behind, but he was too far back to do any damage. Matt jumped and landed. He leaned right and rolled through the second curve.

The two big tabletops were next, and then came the third curve. We'll see if my luck holds, thought Matt, and he pedaled even faster.

The first tabletop was long. Matt landed near the far end, so he pedaled fast to pick up speed for the next jump.

Matt could hear Tyler coming up fast behind him. Matt was two feet away from the curve.

Matt and Tyler entered the curve at the same time. Tyler swung high and Matt swung low. It's shorter this way, Matt thought. I can beat him out of the turn.

But Tyler had other plans. Instead of swinging around the curve, Tyler aimed his bike at Matt. He rode into Matt at full speed. Bam!

Matt's bike was already leaning into the curve, so gravity won and the bike tipped over.

"You lose, Mr. Big Shot," said Tyler. "And I win. I always win." Then Tyler rode away.

Chapter 5

The Main

After the three qualifying races, it was time for the main race of the day. Matt rode up the hill to the starting gate.

"Last again," said Tyler. "You must like being last. Of course, you've had a lot of practice being last today!" Tyler threw back his head and laughed.

Matt closed his eyes and tried to see himself winning.

"If you're going to pray," said Tyler, "you should get down on your knees. Just closing your eyes isn't going to work."

Matt forced himself to breathe in and out very slowly. Then he opened his eyes.

Bang! The gate dropped! The main race had begun!

"Woo-hoo!" yelled Tyler as he rolled down the hill. "I am going to win again!"

We'll see, thought Matt.

As the boys rolled down the hill to jump the three small rolls, Matt moved into last place. Let Tyler think he has me beat, he told himself.

Matt stayed behind the other riders in the first leg of the race.

As they rolled into the first turn, Matt began to speed up just slightly. After the tabletop, he passed rider number five. Now he was fifth and the other boy was last.

The two hills were next. Matt rode next to rider number four in the second turn. Before they reached the two tabletops, Matt passed the other boy.

Matt swung into the third turn in fourth place. Time to speed up and move ahead, he thought.

The three rising jumps were next. Matt poured it on, and with each jump he moved closer and closer to passing the third rider.

The boy in third position kept looking back with a worried look on his face.

Matt was scaring him.

One turn left! Matt pedaled even faster and passed rider number three in the turn. Only two riders were between Matt and the finish line.

This leg of track had four low rolling hills. I have to pass him now, thought Matt. Roll, jump, land! Matt passed the next rider on the second jump. Only Tyler was left.

Tyler turned around and saw Matt.

"Someone has to teach you a lesson," yelled Tyler. And with that, he rammed Matt from the side.

Matt held on, and the bike didn't fall over this time. Tyler swung out his back tire and hit Matt's bike again.

Matt landed crooked but he straightened out and kept riding.

They reached the last small hill before the finish line. Should be easy to get first place now, thought Matt.

Whack!

Tyler pushed Matt off his bike into the fence on the left side of the track.

Crash! Matt hit the fence hard.

Chapter 6

Blood

As the other riders rushed past, Matt stood up. Then he picked up his bike and brushed off the dirt.

My face hurts! Matt touched the sore spot and felt something sticky.

What is that? Blood? I'm bleeding because of Tyler? This is the last straw!

Matt picked up his bike and walked over to the finish line. He stood there and put his hand in the air.

A big burly man Matt had never seen before came over. "What's the fuss, boy?" said the man. "You lost the race."

"Tyler pushed me," said Matt. "He can't do that."

"Don't be a baby," said the man. "Those rules are for the little kids. You're racing with the big boys now."

"The league made those rules," said Matt, "and Tyler has been breaking them all day."

"You've come in last all day," said the man. "You're just a sore loser."

Matt felt the blood dripping down his face. He pressed the cut with his hand to try to stop the bleeding.

"I am a sore loser," said Matt. "I cut my face on the fence because Tyler pushed me!"

Matt held out his bloody hand. "Pushing is a penalty in the rulebook."

"What is it with you and the rules?" said the man.

"When my father was in charge of this track, we followed the rules," said Matt.

"You're dad's not here anymore," said the man. "I'm in charge now. I'll worry about who follows the rules."

"Yeah?" said Matt. "Well, who are you?"

"I'm Jack Mason," he said. "And Tyler happens to be my son."

"This track was in bad shape when
I came, thanks to your father," said
Mason angrily.

"It's all new because of my money,
so I make the rules now, you hear?" He
jabbed Matt in the chest.

"You lost, boy, and that's that," added Mason. Then he turned and walked away with Tyler.

I'm never going to win at this track, thought Matt. Never. I'll never make the racing team, or the state championship, or anything!

Chapter 7

Big Pine

Matt moved his finger down the list of names on the motoboard at the Big Pine Racetrack. The first qualifying race for the state championship took place in the second week of the season.

The track was filled with kids from all over the state. Everyone there wanted to be the state champion.

Will you look at this, thought Matt. Tyler's on another roster.

I won't have to race him until the semifinals, if he makes it, Matt thought. They don't cheat at *this* track.

Matt put on his helmet and then pulled up into lane five. He closed his eyes and imagined himself winning the race.

"Praying again?" said a voice behind him. "It didn't work last time."

Tyler, thought Matt. He's in the next group, so he's waiting behind me.

"Why are you wearing that Evergreen Racing Team shirt, Mr. Big Shot?" said Tyler. "You didn't win a single race at Evergreen last week."

I won this shirt last year, thought Matt, when they didn't allow cheaters at Evergreen.

Matt opened his eyes and looked at the track. I am going to win today, whether you like it or not, Tyler, thought Matt.

Bang! The gate dropped and Matt rode over it. He pedaled fast as he rolled down the hill.

There was another hill right after the starter's hill. Matt rode down the first hill and prepared to jump. He was airborne! There were riders on both sides of him. This is going to be tight, he thought.

Matt turned into the first curve and rode it high.

He rode up another big hill. Up in the air he went. Only one kid was next to him this time.

Matt rode into the second curve.

There's a tabletop ahead, he thought. If I can land toward the end of it, I can pick up some time.

Matt pedaled faster and jumped. He leaned forward as he flew through the air. But the other rider was still next to him.

They rode in the last curve side by side. I have to pull ahead now, or I won't win the race.

Matt rolled out of the final curve and saw the rhythm section, eight small rolling hills right in front of the bleachers.

The other rider is passing me! Better pick it up. Again and again, Matt jumped over the small hills, and with one last blast he crossed the finish line after the other rider.

Chapter 8

Qualifying

Tyler was waiting for Matt in the staging area.

"You came in second in the last moto," said Tyler.

"And?" said Matt.

"And I came in first," said Tyler. "You're not going to be wearing that Evergreen Racing Team shirt very long."

"It's time, boys," said the official. "Which one of you is in this race?"

"I am," said Matt, and he rolled his bike into lane six. But before he could close his eyes to think about the race, bang! The gate dropped.

He did it again! Tyler distracted me.

Down the hill Matt rode. He jumped the first hill. Three riders were already ahead of him by the time he reached the hill at the first turn.

Matt pedaled faster. As he entered the turn, he rolled high to gain momentum. Matt came out of the turn and passed another rider. Two more to go.

Matt picked up speed on the second straightaway. Then he rode up the hill. Matt caught up with the other two riders.

Matt accelerated before the hill. Then he rolled up and jumped. Matt leaned forward trying to gain some ground. Bam! He landed hard. The other two riders were still ahead of him.

Matt entered the third turn behind the two boys. He pedaled faster, but he still couldn't pass them.

Only the rhythm section was left, the eight small hills. Matt tried to pick up speed, but the two boys were faster. Matt pulled up even with one boy after the fourth hill. The other boy passed him up again. Matt crossed the finish line behind the two boys.

"Third!" said Matt. "I came in third! I'm never going to win this way!"

Chapter 9

Three and Counting

Matt saw Tyler waiting for him on the starter's hill. Here we go again. I'll take the offensive this time.

Matt rode up the hill and stopped his bike in front of Tyler. "First place in the last race?" said Matt

"Of course," said Tyler.

"Just checking," said Matt, and he rode over to the starting gate.

"I did some checking too," said Tyler. "You came in third in the last race. You're sliding down, boy."

Matt didn't turn around to answer Tyler. Matt watched the official carefully instead. He didn't want to be caught by surprise like last time.

The official pulled up the gate and glanced at the riders. Then bang! He dropped the gate.

Go, go, go! Matt raced down the starter's hill. Up and over the first hill. Matt jumped the second hill and rode into the first turn.

I'm first this time, thought Matt.

Matt jumped the hill in the second straightaway and went around the third turn. This hill is mine!

As Matt moved into the last turn, he could hear the other riders right behind him.

Only eight small jumps to go! Matt rolled into the rhythm section. He pedaled as fast as he could.

I can't let them beat me now. I have to win state this year, Matt thought.

His tires climbed another hill, then another. Faster and faster he pedaled. He was pedaling so quickly, Matt thought his feet would fly off his legs.

Where's the other hill? thought Matt. Did I already pass it?

People were waving at him and cheering. Matt had crossed the finish line first!

Yes! I am going to the semis!

Chapter 10

The Semis

Three weeks later, only the top four riders from each group raced in the semifinals. Matt was in lane four.

Tyler rode his bike into lane five. He looked at Matt.

"This will be your last race wearing that Evergreen team shirt," Tyler said. "After you lose today, you won't be on the team anymore."

Here we go again, thought Matt.

He closed his eyes and saw himself winning the race. I am going to beat Tyler once and for all.

"I am going to wipe you off the track," said Tyler.

Bang! The gate went down and the race was on. Matt pedaled as fast as he could down the starter's hill.

As he rolled up to the first hill, Matt slowed up a bit. I'll let Tyler think he's winning. Then I can come from behind and beat him!

Tyler jumped the hill just before Matt and pulled ahead.

"See ya!" yelled Tyler.

Another boy pulled up next to Matt, but Matt sped up so the boy couldn't pass him.

Second place is far enough back.

Matt jumped the second hill and rolled into the first curve.

He stayed right behind Tyler. They flew over the next hill, and Matt landed behind Tyler.

Matt and Tyler rolled into the third turn. The tabletop was next. Time to make my move, thought Matt.

Matt pedaled faster and then jumped. He pulled up alongside Tyler in midair. Tyler swung his back tire to hit Matt. Matt pulled his bike to the right, and Tyler missed!

Matt pulled ahead of Tyler.

"Hey!" yelled Tyler, and he rammed Matt's bike from behind.

Matt held on tight and jumped the hill before the final curve. As he swung into the final curve, Tyler rammed into him again.

Matt was leaning into the curve, so he almost fell off the bike.

Before Matt could get control of the bike, three riders passed him. Matt rode out of the curve and tried to catch up. He rode over the eight small hills as fast as he could, but it wasn't enough. He didn't pass a single rider.

Only the top four go to the final, and I came in fifth! And Tyler won again. I am not doing this again. I am not going to lose because Tyler cheated.

Matt stood at the finish line and raised his hand.

Chapter 11

Fair Play

"I'm number one," yelled Tyler as he rode his bike in circles at the finish line. "I'm number one!"

Matt watched as Tyler's dad came out of the bleachers and gave him a high-five. Then an official came up to Matt.

"I see you have your hand up," said the official. "What can I do for you?"

"I want to report a violation," said Matt.

"Okay," said the official, "let me write it down." He took a pencil and small notebook out of his pocket.

"Your name is?" asked the official.

"Matthew Daniels," said Matt.

"Daniels, huh?" said the official and he wrote it down. "I'm Mr. Bosch, by the way. As for what happened, well, I saw it with my own two eyes."

"Oh," said Matt.

"How's your dad?" said Mr. Bosch. "I hear he's overseas."

"Yes, sir, he is," said Matt.

"You taking care of your mom?" asked Mr. Bosch.

"Yes, sir," said Matt.

"Good," said Mr. Bosch.

"Now let's take care of this situation," he added. "You stay here. I'll be right back."

Mr. Bosch walked over to Tyler and his dad and started talking.

"That was not a violation!" yelled Tyler's dad.

Matt looked over at the bleachers. Oh no! Mom is coming over!

"He's just a sore loser," yelled Tyler's dad. Three other officials came over to Tyler and his dad, but Matt couldn't hear what the officials were saying.

Matt's mom came up to him. "What's this all about?" she asked.

"He was cheating," said Matt, "so I reported him."

Matt's mom touched the cut on his cheek. "Did he cheat last week, too?" she asked.

"Yes," said Matt.

"What do you mean, Tyler's out?" yelled Tyler's dad. "My boy came in first. He won! You can't let that whiner race in my boy's place."

Tyler's dad turned around and walked over to Matt. Tyler followed him.

"You stole my boy's place," said Tyler's dad, and he jabbed Matt in the chest.

"Just wait until you come back to Evergreen. We're going to teach you a lesson!" said Tyler.

"That's enough!" said another official.

"I'm not going back," said Matt.

"Don't you touch my boy," said Matt's mom.

"You'll have to leave, Mr. Mason," said Mr. Bosch.

"You can't kick me off this track!" said Tyler's dad. "I have a right to be here."

"Our riders don't cheat at Big Pine," said Mr. Bosch. "And when you pushed a rider, you crossed over the line. You have to go or I'm calling the police."

"Let me help you to your car," said another official, and he turned Tyler's dad to face the parking lot.

"I'm going, I'm going," said Tyler's dad. Then he yelled, "Hurry up, Tyler!"

"I'm coming," said Tyler.

Chapter 12

Qualified

"Thank you, Mr. Bosch," Matt's mom said to the official.

"No problem," said Mr. Bosch. "We've worked with your husband many times over at Evergreen."

"He would never tolerate cheating," said Matt's mom.

"We don't either," said Mr. Bosch. "You're welcome to join our racing family here at Big Pine."

"We accept," said Matt. Matt's mother smiled.

Mr. Bosch looked around at the crowd. "Okay, everyone," he said. "Let's get back to racing!" Then he turned to Matt. "And you, young man, need a new jersey."

Matt looked down at his green and black Evergreen Racing Team jersey. He'd won a lot of races with this jersey, but now it was time to join a new team.

"I think we have one in your size in the booth," said Mr. Bosch. "Let's go and take a look."

Matt and his mom followed Mr. Bosch to the official's booth.

"How much for the jersey?" asked Matt's mom.

"Your husband has helped us here at Big Pine many times," said Mr. Bosch. "Let's just call it even."

Matt looked up at his mom and smiled.

Mr. Bosch dug in the boxes on the shelf. "Ah, here it is." He pulled out a green and gold shirt and gave it to Matt.

Matt put on the new shirt

"Looks good," said Mr. Bosch. "Now go out there and win one for Big Pine!"

"Yes, sir," said Matt. He rode his bike up to the starter's hill.

He closed his eyes one last time. See yourself winning, Dad always said. In his mind's eye, Matt saw himself crossing the finish line first. Then he opened his eyes.

Bang! The gate dropped.

Matt rode down the starter's hill. He rolled up to the second hill. Three other riders were right beside him.

Matt rode up the hill in front of the first turn. As he jumped, the other three riders jumped with him.

Matt leaned forward, trying to gain some ground.

Matt rolled in the first turn, high on the curve. Matt pedaled as fast as he could as he rolled out of the turn. He passed one rider.

Matt rolled up the hill and jumped. Two riders jumped with him.

All three riders turned into the curve together. Matt rode the curve high.

As he came out of the turn he was just ahead of a rider with a red shirt.

Matt pedaled faster as he approached the tabletop. Matt sailed over it. He landed ahead of the red-shirt rider.

Only one more to go, thought Matt. But as Matt jumped the hill before the final turn, the rider in the red shirt caught up with him. Matt and the two other riders rode in to the final turn together.

Matt pulled out of the turn even with the other riders. The people in the bleachers were cheering as the riders came onto the final stretch of track.

Six jumps to go and a rider in a blue shirt pulled ahead. Matt pedaled faster.

He pulled even with the rider in the blue shirt. Now he had to pass him.

The red shirt rider pulled ahead of both of them. Now Matt was third.

Matt pushed himself to pass the rider with the blue shirt again.

Matt pulled even with the rider in the red shirt. On the last jump, the blue-shirt rider pulled ahead of Matt.

Only ten meters to go!

Matt pedaled faster and pulled even with the rider in the blue shirt.

Matt gave a final burst of speed. He inched ahead of the rider.

Finish line!

I won!

About the Author

Anastasia Suen is the author of more than seventy books for young people. She spent countless hours riding her bike as a child. Anastasia grew up in Florida in the early NASA days and now lives with her family in Plano, Texas.

About the Illustrator

When Sean Tiffany was growing up, he lived on a small island off the coast of Maine. Every day, from sixth grade until he graduated from high school, he had to take a boat to get to school. When Sean isn't working on his art, he works on a multimedia project called "OilCan Drive," which combines music and art. He has a pet cactus named Jim.

Glossary

accelerate (ak-SEL-uh-rate)—to get faster and faster

airborne (AIR born)—up in the air

champion (CHAM-pee-uhn)—the winner of a competition

competition (kom-puh-TISH-uhn)—a contest of some kind

jersey (JUR-zee)—a shirt, usually a shirt worn as part of a sports uniform

momentum (moh-MEN-tuhm)—the speed an object has when it is moving

moto (MOH-toe)—a race

ram (ram)—to crash into something with great force

roster (RAHSS-tur)—a list

violate (VYE-uh-late)—to break a rule

A BMX Bike

See the ABA Rule Book: http://www.ababmx.com/

1. 20 inch tires
Slicks are tires with smooth edges.
Knobbies are tires with ridges and bumps.

2. high handlebars

3. light, strong frame

4. single gear

5. shin guards

6. safety helmet
Helmets are padded on the inside to protect the rider's head and face.
Some helmets have air vents to keep the rider cool.

Discussion Questions

1. Do you think Tyler was really a championship rider?

2. Was Tyler's dad playing fair by ignoring the rules for the older kids?

3. Do you think Matt made the right decision when he reported the violations?

Writing Prompts

1. What would you do if you were in a competition with a bully?

2. Write about a race you have ridden or run in.

3. What do you think happened at the BMX races the next week, after the story ends?

Internet Sites

Do you want to know more about subjects related to this book? Or are you interested in learning about other topics? Then check out FactHound, a fun, easy way to find Internet sites.

Our investigative staff has already sniffed out great sites for you!

Here's how to use FactHound:

1. Visit *www.facthound.com*.

2. Select your grade level.

3. To learn more about subjects related to this book, type in the book's ISBN number: **159889059X**.

4. Click the **Fetch It** button.

FactHound will fetch the best Internet sites for you!